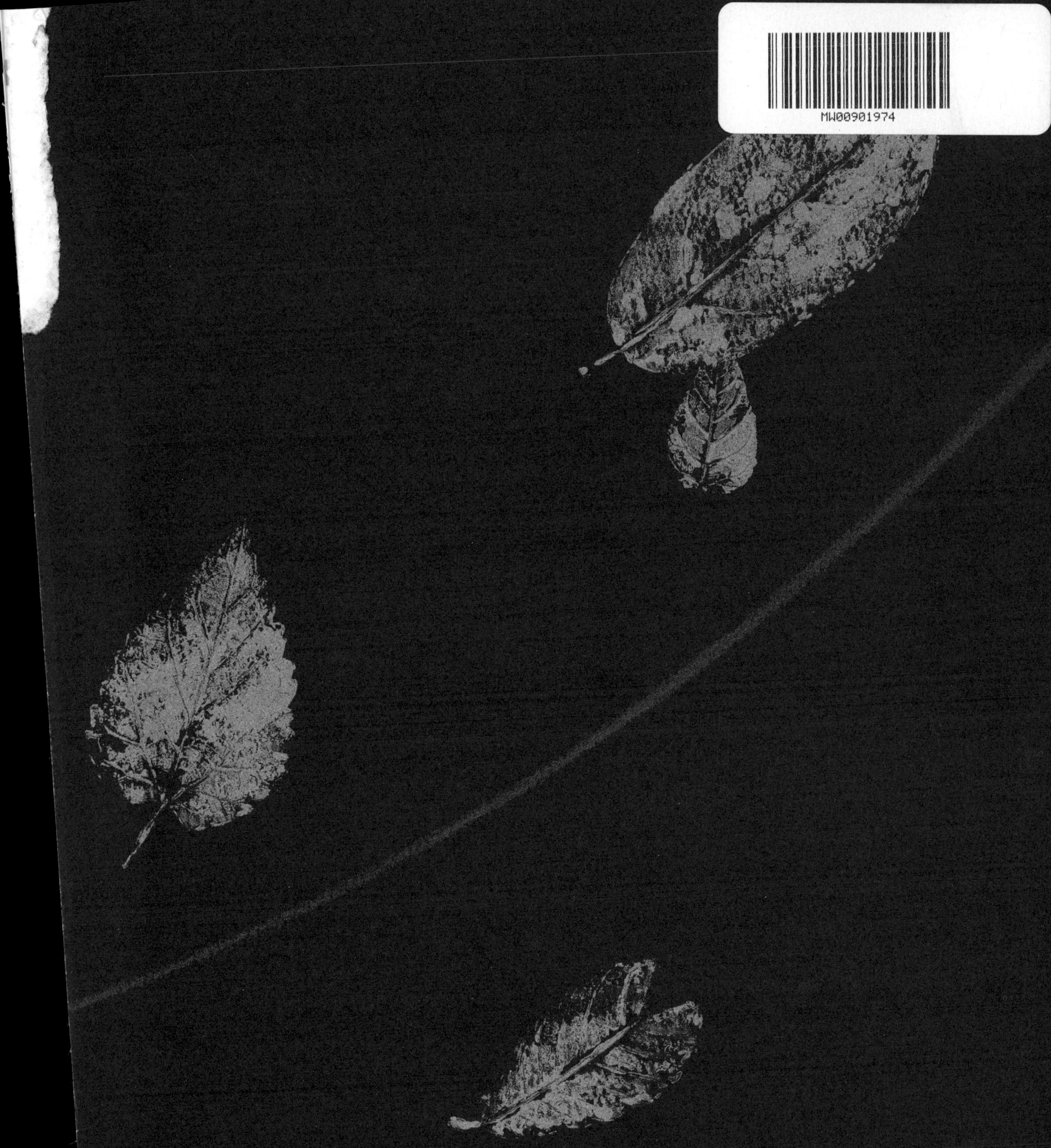
MW00901974

A WILD WINDY NIGHT

YUI ABE

MUSEYON
NEW YORK

Whoosh Whoosh

"It's so windy tonight, Ricky . . ."

"Mom, Mr. Wind is crying out . . . please, come play with me."

"That's right. But it's time for you to go to bed."

Whoosh-Whoosh-Ka-whoosh

The wind grew stronger and stronger.

Rattle-rattle. Ricky's windows shook.

Whoo-o-o-o-sh!

Suddenly, the wind howled very loudly.

"Oh, NO!"

"There goes my car!"

REO

Then
all the toys
jumped

into the wind!

“Wait,

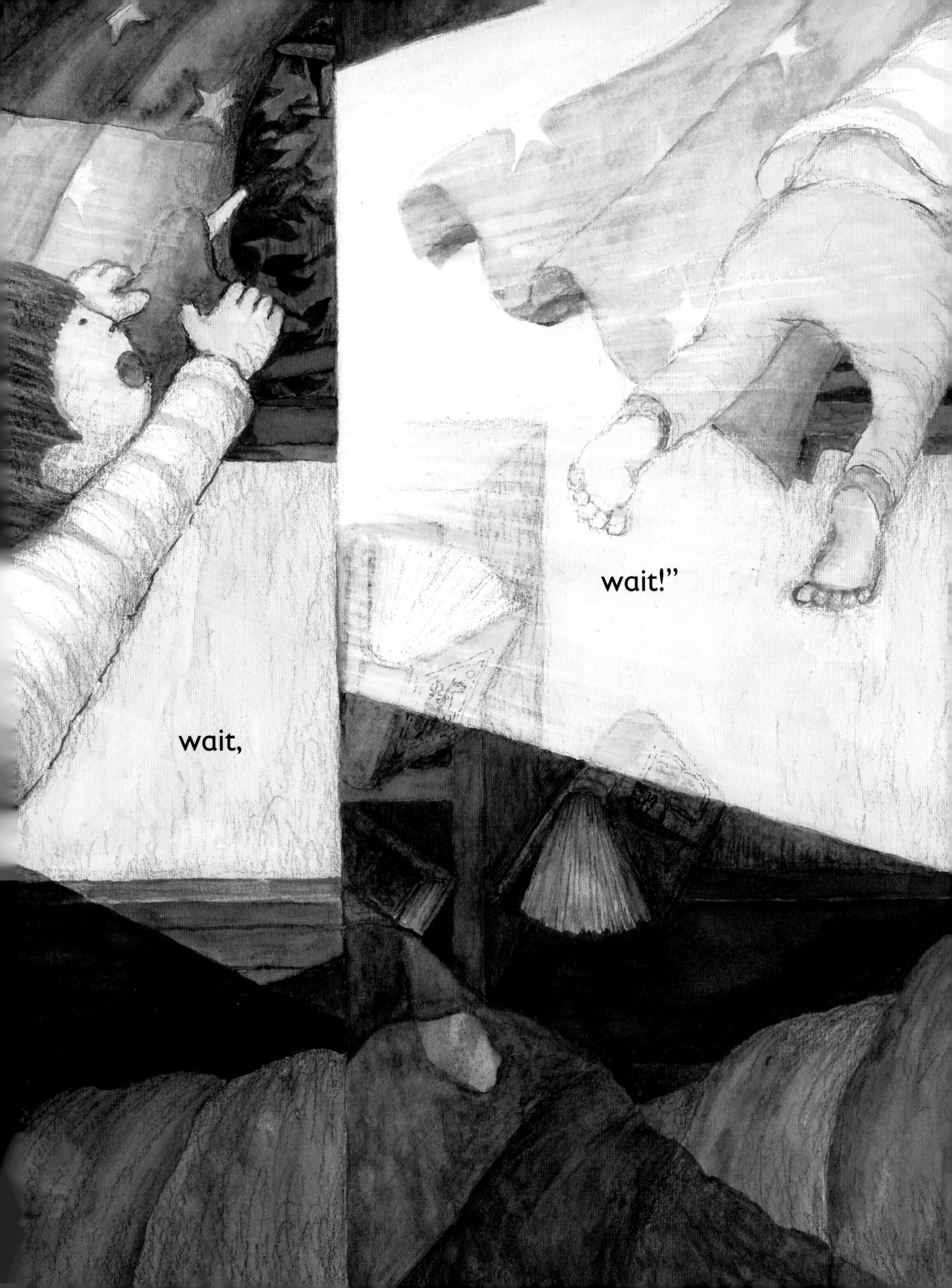

wait,

wait!”

Whoosh-Whoosh.
KA-WHOOSH!

Swish
Swoosh

Wish-Whoosh

"Let's race to the forest over there! Ready, set, go!"

Whoosh-whoosh ka-whoosh!

"Everyone shout out, louder than Mr. Wind!"

SWISH-SWOOSH-KA-WHOOSH!

"Hey, let's play hide-and-seek here.
Mr. Wind, you be the first seeker.
I'll count to ten . . . then you come and find us!"

"One.
Two.
Three.
Four.
Five.
Six.

Seven.
Eight.
Nine . . .

Ten! Now come find us!”

Rustle rustle rustle . . .
"Shhh, Mr. Wind is coming
this way."
Rustle rustle rustle . . .
"Hey, Don't come out yet. Stay"
Whoosh

Whoosh whoosh whoosh . . .
"Oh, NO!"

WHOO-O-O-O-SH!

"Everyone, everyone flew away.
I'm still hiding, all alone.
Mr. Wind come find me quick!"

Just then . . .

SWOOSH-HEE-HEE

The wind blew playfully as it laughed at me.

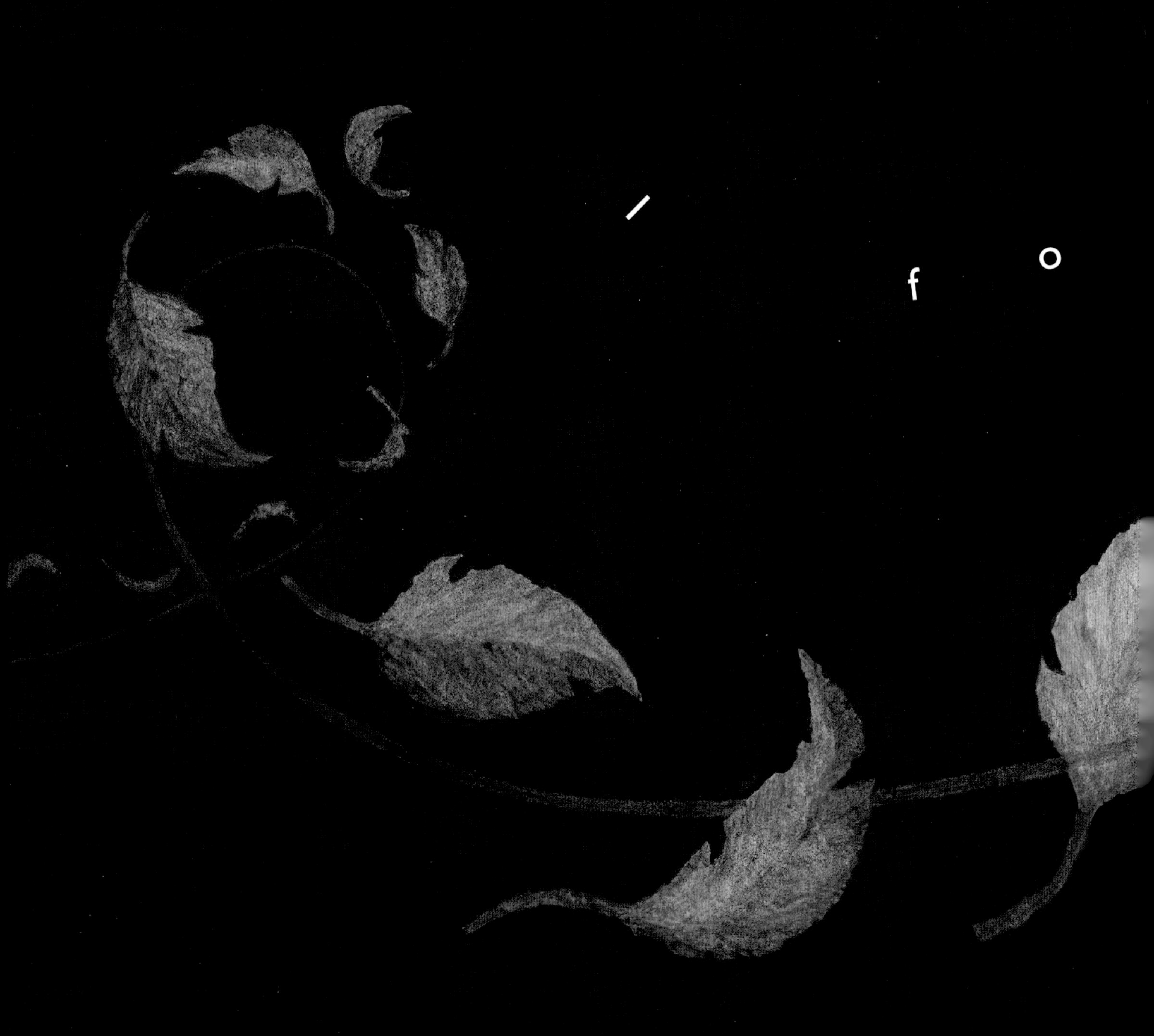

und you.

"Ricky!"

“Mom!”

"What are you doing here?"

“We were playing hide-and-seek together in the forest, but then Mr. Wind found us and blew us all the way here!”

"What? Where's Mr. Wind?"

"Is he hiding?"

"Look, Ricky. The window is open. Shall we take a look outside?"

"Mr. Wind isn't anywhere."

"I'm sure he got tired and went home to rest. He'll come back to play another day. Now it's our turn to sleep, Ricky. Good night."

About Author

Yui Abe was born in Miyagi, Japan in 1986. Growing up, she was influenced by her father who was a painter and a junior high school art teacher, and developed a love for drawing from a young age. She studied illustration and picture book creation in Tokyo, and has since worked on book cover illustrations and promotional art for theater productions. Her illustration works include "The Wonder Maps of the World" (Asahi Shimbun Publications) and "Onibaba's Island" (Shogakukan). Yui currently lives in Tokyo.

A WILD WINDY NIGHT

Alexandrea Mallia, translator.

Published in the United States and Canada by:
Museyon Inc.
2322 30th Road
LIC, NY 11102

Museyon is a registered trademark.
Visit us online at www.museyon.com

First published in Japan in 2021 by Poplar Publishing Co., Ltd.
English translation rights arranged with Poplar Publishing Co., Ltd.

Library of Congress Cataloging-in-Publication Data available.

ISBN 978-1-940842-74-5

Printed in China